THE
BIG,
BAD
BULLY

Jack Canfield &
Miriam Laundry

With illustrations by Eva Morales

Health Communications, Inc.
Boca Raton, Florida

www.hcibooks.com

**Library of Congress Cataloging-in-Publication Data
is available through the Library of Congress**

© 2019 Jack Canfield and Miriam Laundry

ISBN-13: 978-07573-2308-9 (Hardcover)
ISBN-10: 07573-2308-1 (Hardcover)
ISBN-13: 978-07573-2309-6 (ePub)
ISBN-10: 07573-2309-X (ePub)

Publisher: Health Communications, Inc.
      1700 NW 2nd Avenue
      Boca Raton, FL 33432-1653

Miriam Laundry photo by Nicole Arnt Photography & Design
Interior formatting by Lawna Patterson Oldfield

*This book is dedicated to all those
who wish to be free to
be themselves.*

—Jack Canfield

*Dedicated to my children:
Sarina, Alissa, Aiden and Lucas.
You are my WHY.*

—Miriam Laundry

"Pigtails are for babies!" she snarled at me.

Her words hurt more than the
time I broke my arm.

I quickly untied my hair.
I wore my hair down for the
rest of the school year.

That was the first time I met
the Big, Bad Bully. I was in the
second grade.

I am not sure where she came from.
I had never noticed her at school
before. But she noticed me . . .

...grade 4...

...and grade 5.

She called me names like "fatty," "piglet," and "ugly."

Things are worse now that I am in the 6th grade. Even when I don't see her, I can always hear the whispers, the giggles, and the growls.

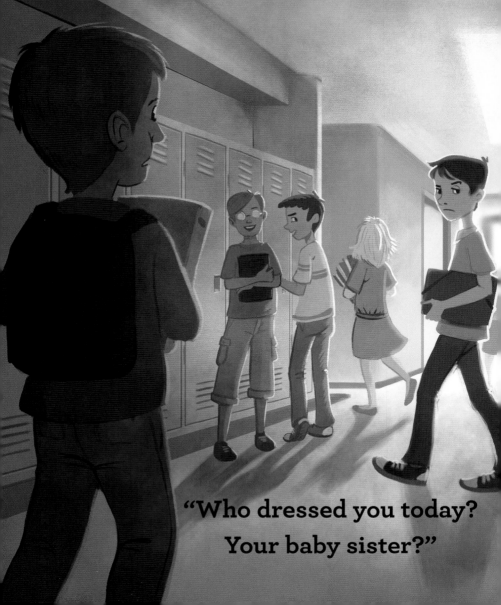

"Who dressed you today? Your baby sister?"

Many nights, I cry myself to sleep.
How can someone be so cruel?

Doesn't she know that words hurt?

I don't know what to do anymore.

I have to put a stop to this, but
I am weak when Bully is around.

"Tomorrow is MY day,"
I tell myself.

But . . .

I woke up ready.

I ate a good breakfast...

...and headed to school.

I knew I would find her in the girls' bathroom like I usually did.

I was going to put an end to this once and for all.

I quietly opened the bathroom door and took one slow step inside.

"I am brave,"
I told myself.

"I CAN do this,"
I whispered.

I looked up and there she stood,
right in front of me.

A lump formed in my throat
when our eyes met.

I was about to say something,
but I stopped myself.

Instead, I looked deep into her eyes,
and that's when I saw her.
Really saw her. For the first time.

The End Beginning

A New Beginning: Overcoming the Bully in the Mirror

We all know that the words others say to us can either lift us as high as the clouds or drop us down like a crashing plane. But what about the words we tell ourselves? What about that inner voice we always have going on?

What we say to ourselves impacts us even more than what others say to us!

We all want to stop bullying. We cringe at the words *baby, fatty, piglet, ugly, zit face.* But what about the words "you are not good enough," "nobody loves you," or "loser"?

These are all unacceptable things to say to others...but why is it okay for us to say them to ourselves?

Why is that acceptable?

It seems that the kindest words should be whispered to ourselves. "You're beautiful! You're smart! You're precious!

You're perfect just the way you are!"

What if we looked in the mirror and started to appreciate ourselves?

What if, instead of pointing out our flaws, we started to look at the greatness in us?

What if we were kind to ourselves?

How powerful would that be?

What do *you* say when you look in the mirror?

The Positive Mirror Exercise

The mirror exercise is a simple, yet powerful self-esteem and self-confidence building exercise that you can do yourself. Its purpose is to replace the normal negative self-talk that dominates our thoughts with positive, self-affirming self-talk. It's an exercise that should be performed every night for at least forty days in a row.

Every night before going to bed, stand in front of a mirror and appreciate yourself for all that you accomplished during the day. Look deep into your eyes and just hold that eye contact for a few seconds.

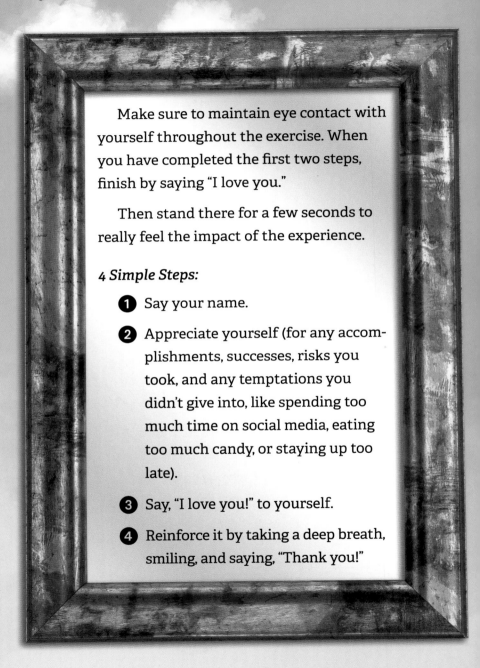

Make sure to maintain eye contact with yourself throughout the exercise. When you have completed the first two steps, finish by saying "I love you."

Then stand there for a few seconds to really feel the impact of the experience.

4 *Simple Steps:*

1. Say your name.

2. Appreciate yourself (for any accomplishments, successes, risks you took, and any temptations you didn't give into, like spending too much time on social media, eating too much candy, or staying up too late).

3. Say, "I love you!" to yourself.

4. Reinforce it by taking a deep breath, smiling, and saying, "Thank you!"

For Parents and Teachers Who Want More

There are a number of exercises and activities you can do to reinforce the habit of positive self-talk and self-affirmation promoted in this book, which will contribute greatly to your children's self-esteem.

1 Encourage your kids to do the 4 Simple Steps in the Positive Mirror Exercise. If you are a parent, you can stand beside your child and give them prompts about their positive qualities and characteristics that they may have overlooked to then say to themselves in the mirror. You can also demonstrate the exercise by doing it first and showing them how it is done. Be aware that the older the child the more awkward or embarrassing it might be at first. But over time, they will get used to it. Encourage them to make this a lifetime habit. One of our friends has done this exercise every night for more than seven years.

If you are a teacher, print out the instructions for this exercise and send it home to the parents with a note that you are asking the parents to encourage or monitor their child to make sure to do this exercise for the next forty days as a way to bolster and improve their self-esteem and self-confidence. Make sure to tell them that the whole class is being assigned this exercise so they don't think you are singling out their child as having a self-esteem problem.

2 Have the kids make a written list of all their positive qualities, skills, and attributes.

3 Have them write their name vertically down the left side of a page and then come up with a positive word that describes them that starts with the letters in their name. For example:

Joyful	**M**agnificent	**H**ard-working
Athletic	**I**nventive	**E**nthusiastic
Confident	**R**adiant	**A**ppreciative
Kind	**I**nspiring	**T**alented
	Artistic	**H**appy
	Musical	**E**fficient
		Resourceful

A great resource for this is to type *"adjectives starting with A to describe a person"* into your browser. It will take you to *www.AdjectivesStarting.com,* which contains a lengthy list of adjectives for every letter of the alphabet.

4 Ask your kids to answer the following questions at dinner every night:

- Tell me about one thing you learned in school today.
- What did you do for someone else at school today?
- What was your greatest success today?
- What are you looking forward to tomorrow?

5 This one is for teachers. (Parents with several children could also do this with the parents included in the exercise.) Give the students a sheet of paper with a list of all students' names in the class on it. Ask them to think about the nicest thing they could say about each of their classmates and write it down next to their name. Later, take the time to write down the name of each student on a separate piece of paper and list what each child has said about that person. Then give back each student his or her list. This is a very powerful exercise.

To see just how powerful this exercise is, read the story "All the Good Things" in *Chicken Soup for the Soul®* by Jack Canfield and Mark Victor Hansen.

5 One more thing, it's important to get in the habit of filling our minds with positivity in the form of self-affirmations. The following are some suggestions to pass along to your children and students.

- It's recommended that you use affirmations on a daily basis, much like a one-a-day multi-vitamin tablet for the mind. This will build the internal mental strength to replace all negative input with a positive affirmation.

- You can write your affirmations on a 3x5 card and tape it to your bathroom mirror or on your bedroom wall. You can have them pop up on your phone as reminders or on your tablet.

- Repeat your affirmations twice per day. The best times are first thing in the morning and around bedtime.

Here are some tips on writing effective affirmations:

- Affirmations should always be in the present tense. Start with "I am…"

- Affirmations should always be stated in the positive

- Affirmations should be short and to the point

Some examples:

I am beautiful

I am a strong person

I am courageous

I am intelligent

I am loved

When you are repeating your affirmations make sure you are allowing the words to sink in and feeling the emotions of what those words mean.

About the Authors

Jack Canfield is the cocreator of the #1 *New York Times* bestselling *Chicken Soup for the Soul®* book series including *Chicken Soup for the Kid's Soul, Chicken Soup for the Preteen Soul, Chicken Soup for the Girl's Soul* and *Chicken Soup for the Parent's Soul*. He started his career as a teacher in the Chicago Public Schools and later became a leading expert in the area of teaching teachers and parents how to build and maintain high self-esteem in children of all ages. He is the coauthor of *100 Ways to Enhance Self-Concept in Classroom* and *Self-Esteem in the Classroom*, and is also a co-founder and past board member of the National Council for Self-Esteem, which honored him with their National Leadership Award.

Jack is currently the founder and chairman of the Canfield Training Group in Santa Barbara, California. He conducts workshops and trainings on how to become more successful in every area of your life based on his bestselling book *The Success Principles™: How to Get from Where You Are to Where You Want to Be*. His current mission is to train one million people to teach these principles and practices by 2030.

Jack is the author or coauthor of more than 200 books that have been published in 49 languages around the world, and he is a Guinness Book World Record Holder for having 7 books on the *New York Times* bestseller list on the same day.

Jack has been seen by millions of viewers on national television shows such as *Larry King Live, The Oprah Winfrey Show, Oprah's Super Soul Sunday, Montel, The Today Show, Fox and Friends, the NBC Nightly News*, and the *CBS Evening News* shows.

You can learn more about Jack and his work at *www.JackCanfield.com* and at *www.facebook.com/JackCanfield Fan* and at *www.youtube.com/jackcanfield*.

Miriam Laundry is a sought-after educational speaker, writing mentor, and author who travels the country sharing her positive I CAN message. Schools seek her out to inspire their students through her I CAN children's book series or to engage older children with her TEDx Talk, "The Bully in the Mirror." The I CAN series includes: *I CAN Believe in Myself, I CAN Make a Difference,* and *I CAN Be Me.* She set a Guinness World Record™ in 2014 for the largest online book discussion in a 24-hour period. More than 100,000 children and adults from 29 countries participated in this record with the purpose of promoting positive mental health. Her books have received numerous book awards, including Mom's Choice Award and Readers' Favorite International Award. Miriam was awarded the 2014 Winspiration Award for her contribution in empowering children worldwide.

Miriam lives in the beautiful Niagara region in Canada with her husband and four children. When she isn't writing, you can find her cheering her kids on at sporting events, music competitions, or working hard at her second job—taxi driver for her children. (Tips always appreciated.)

Miriam enjoys mentoring aspiring authors who have an empowering children's message to share. She draws her inspiration from a desire to equip her children with the best tools for living a fulfilled life. She wrote the first draft of her first book on the flight back from a Jack Canfield event. Miriam spent the week being inspired by Jack's teachings and kept thinking, "I wish I had known this when I was a child." The award-winning, bestselling book, *I CAN Believe in Myself,* came from that initial instinct. She continues to share those same inspiring principles with her children and strives to inspire many more.

You can learn more about Miriam and her work at *www.MiriamLaundry.com* and at *www.facebook.com/ MiriamLaundryFanPage* as well as *www.Instagram.com/ Miriam.Laundry.*